GRAPHIC MYTHICAL CREATURES

UNICORNS

BY GARY JEFFREY

ILLUSTRATED BY DHEERAJ VERMA

Gareth Stevens
Publishing

Please visit our website, www.garethstevens.com.
For a free color catalog of all our high-quality books,
call toll free 1-800-542-2595 or fax 1-877-542-2596.

Library of Congress Cataloging-in-Publication Data

Jeffrey, Gary.
Unicorns / Gary Jeffrey.
p. cm. — (Graphic mythical creatures)
Includes index.
ISBN 978-1-4339-6769-6 (pbk.)
ISBN 978-1-4339-6770-2 (6-pack)
ISBN 978-1-4339-6767-2 (library binding)
1. Unicorns—Juvenile literature. I. Title.
GR830.U6J44 2012
398.24'54—dc23
2011025303

First Edition

Published in 2012 by
Gareth Stevens Publishing
111 East 14th Street, Suite 349
New York, NY 10003

Copyright © 2012 David West Books

Designed by David West Books

Printed in China

CPSIA compliance information: Batch #DW12GS: For further information contact Gareth Stevens, New York, New York at 1-800-542-2595.

CONTENTS

Horn of Plenty

The legendary unicorn first showed up in ancient texts on natural history. Scholars based their descriptions on travelers' tales and noted unicorns for their wildness and the special properties of their horns.

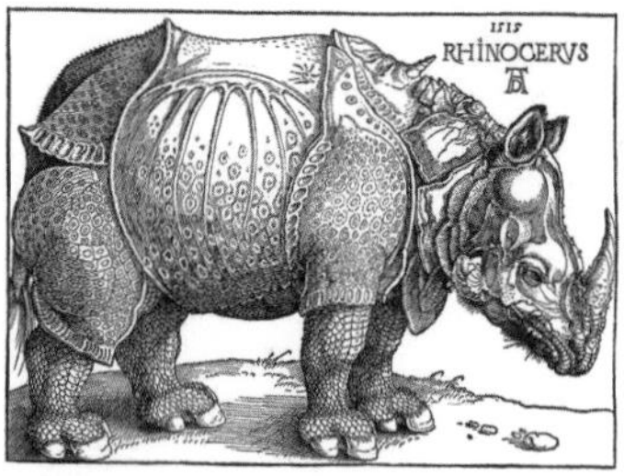
1515
RHINOCERVS

Travelers' tales of the Indian rhinoceros may have given rise to the idea of unicorns.

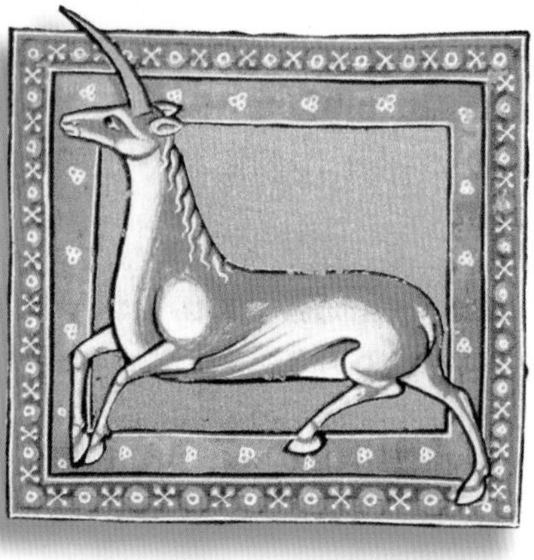

A "monocerous" in a 13th-century illuminated bestiary

The Purifier

The classic unicorn was a horse-like animal with a goat beard, cloven hoofs, and a lion's tail. In legends, it used its long, spiralling horn to purify water for all the other woodland beasts.

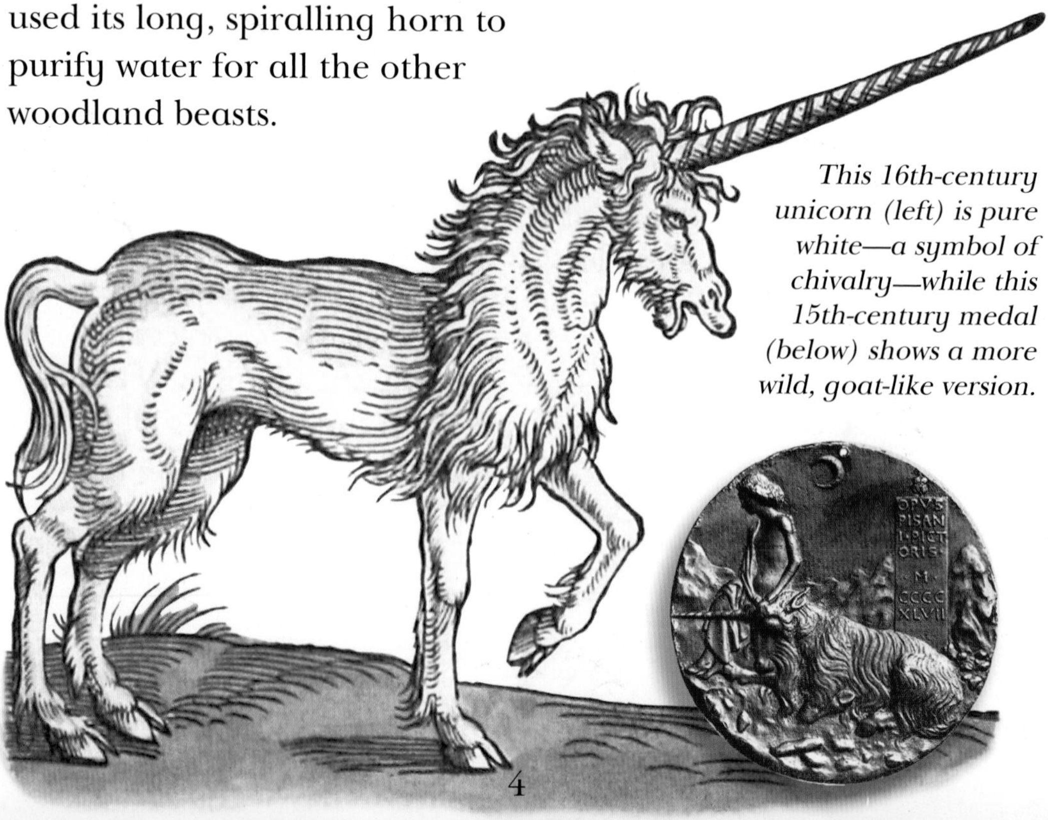
OPVS
PISANI
PICTORIS
M
CCCC
XLVII

This 16th-century unicorn (left) is pure white—a symbol of chivalry—while this 15th-century medal (below) shows a more wild, goat-like version.

Magic Horn

Unicorn horn, or alicorn, was said to show up or neutralize poisons and was much sought after by unpopular rulers. Supposed alicorns were actually narwhal tusks and were made into drinking cups.

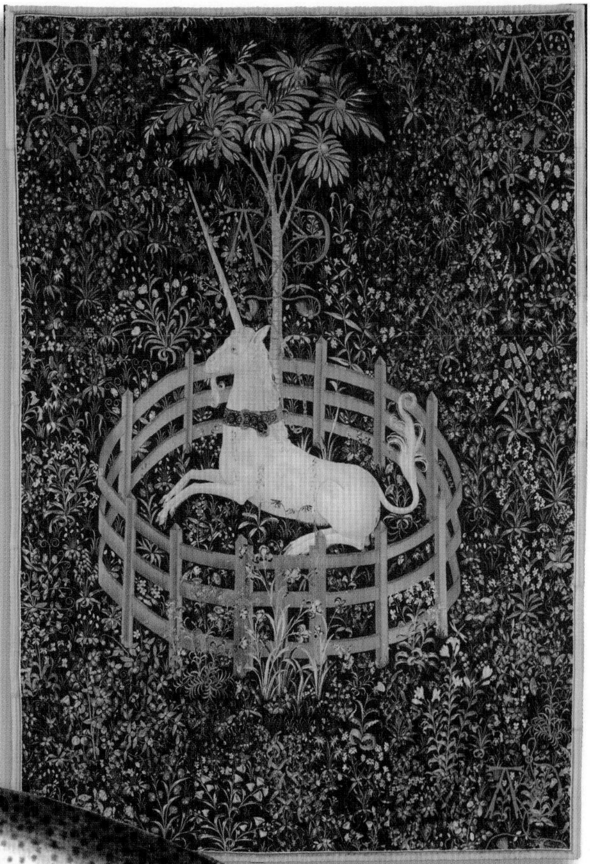

A tapestry showing a captured unicorn. The unicorn hunt was a popular subject during the Renaissance.

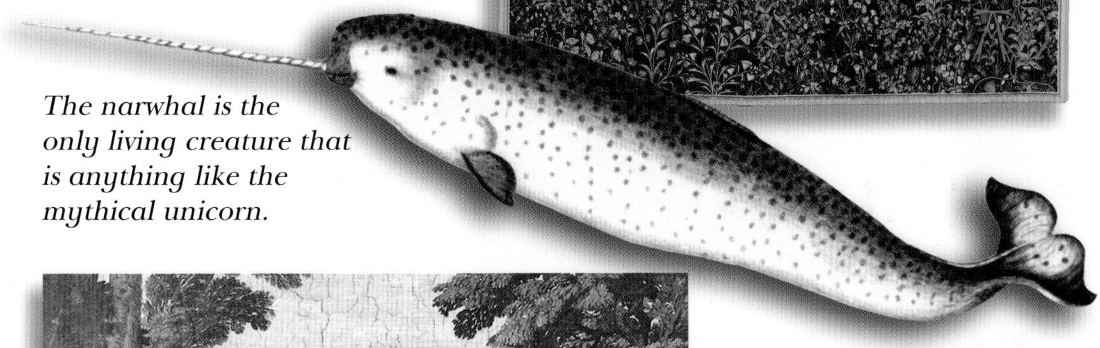

The narwhal is the only living creature that is anything like the mythical unicorn.

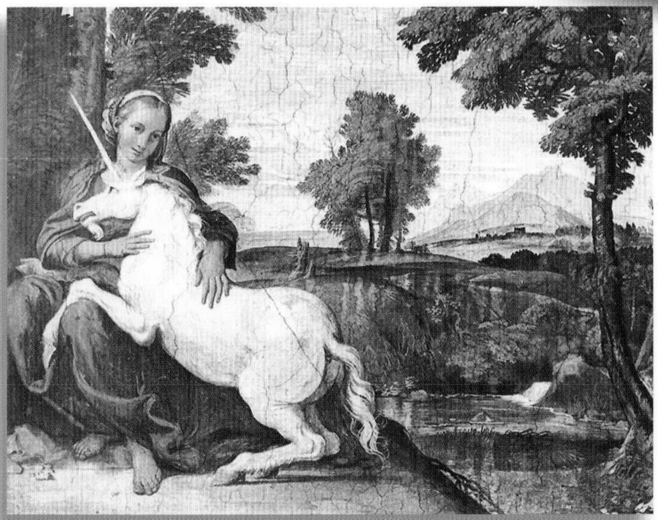

A unicorn lies tame in the arms of a maiden.

The Noble Unicorn

In lore, a unicorn could only be lured and captured using a pure maiden. Unicorns came to represent the virtues of faithfulness and purity in art and on coats of arms.

Therese and the Unicorn

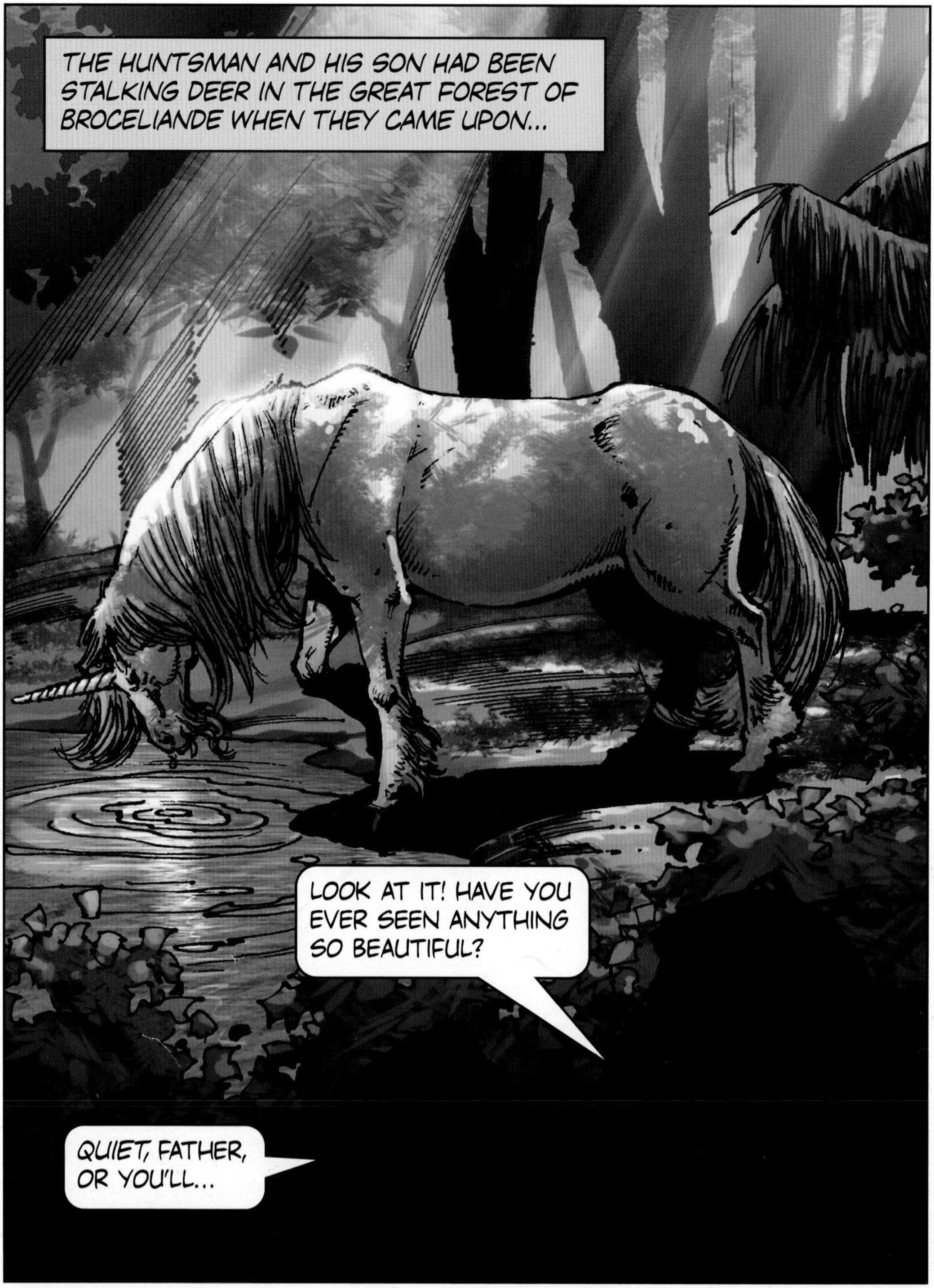

THE HUNTSMAN AND HIS SON HAD BEEN STALKING DEER IN THE GREAT FOREST OF BROCELIANDE WHEN THEY CAME UPON...
LOOK AT IT! HAVE YOU EVER SEEN ANYTHING SO BEAUTIFUL?
QUIET, FATHER, OR YOU'LL...

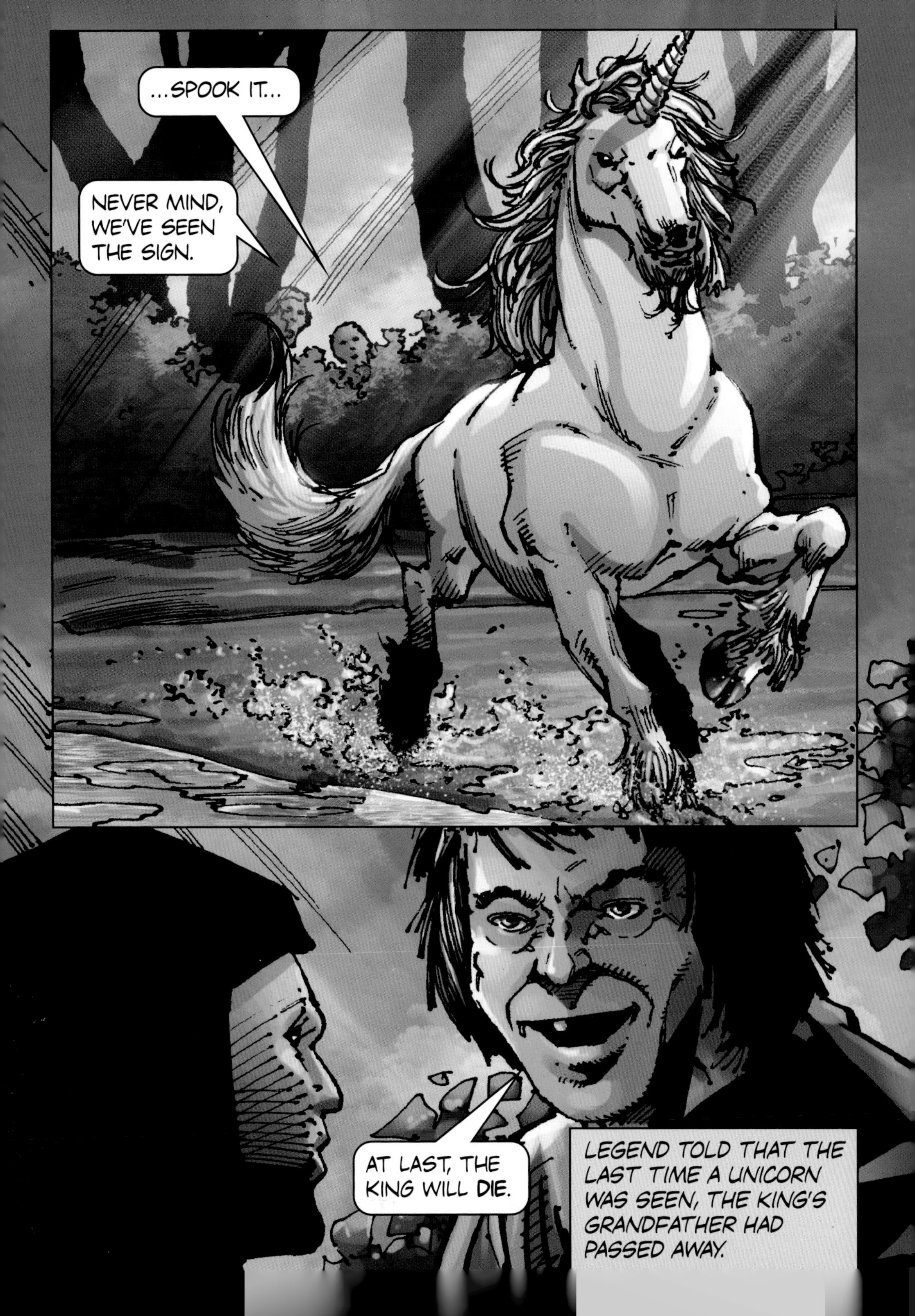
...SPOOK IT...
NEVER MIND, WE'VE SEEN THE SIGN.
AT LAST, THE KING WILL DIE.
LEGEND TOLD THAT THE LAST TIME A UNICORN WAS SEEN, THE KING'S GRANDFATHER HAD PASSED AWAY.

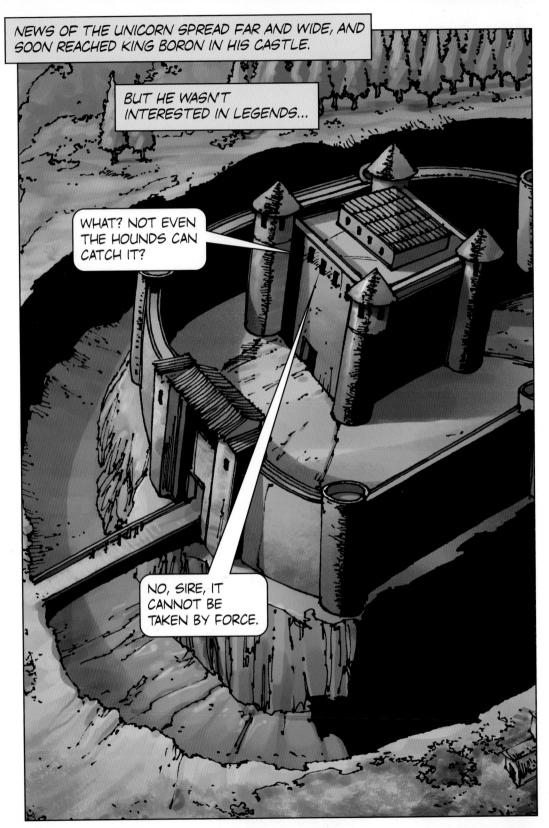

NEWS OF THE UNICORN SPREAD FAR AND WIDE, AND SOON REACHED KING BORON IN HIS CASTLE.

BUT HE WASN'T INTERESTED IN LEGENDS...

WHAT? NOT EVEN THE HOUNDS CAN CATCH IT?

NO, SIRE, IT CANNOT BE TAKEN BY FORCE.

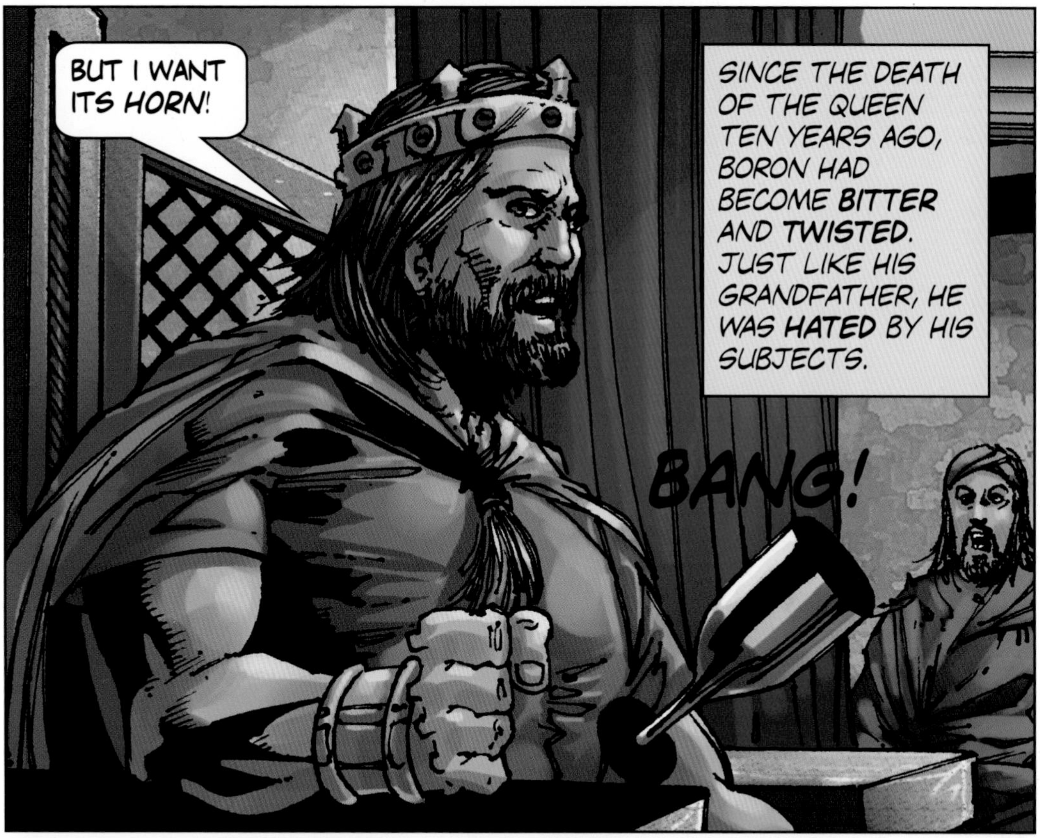
BUT I WANT ITS HORN!
SINCE THE DEATH OF THE QUEEN TEN YEARS AGO, BORON HAD BECOME BITTER AND TWISTED. JUST LIKE HIS GRANDFATHER, HE WAS HATED BY HIS SUBJECTS.
BANG!

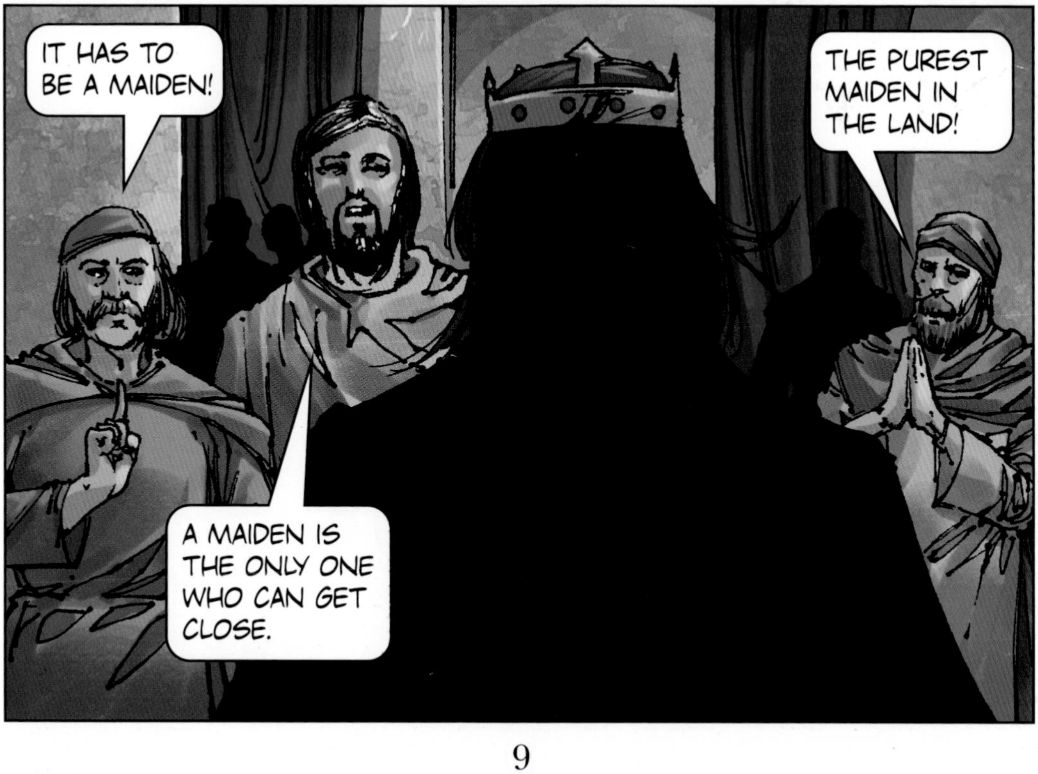
IT HAS TO BE A MAIDEN!
A MAIDEN IS THE ONLY ONE WHO CAN GET CLOSE.
THE PUREST MAIDEN IN THE LAND!

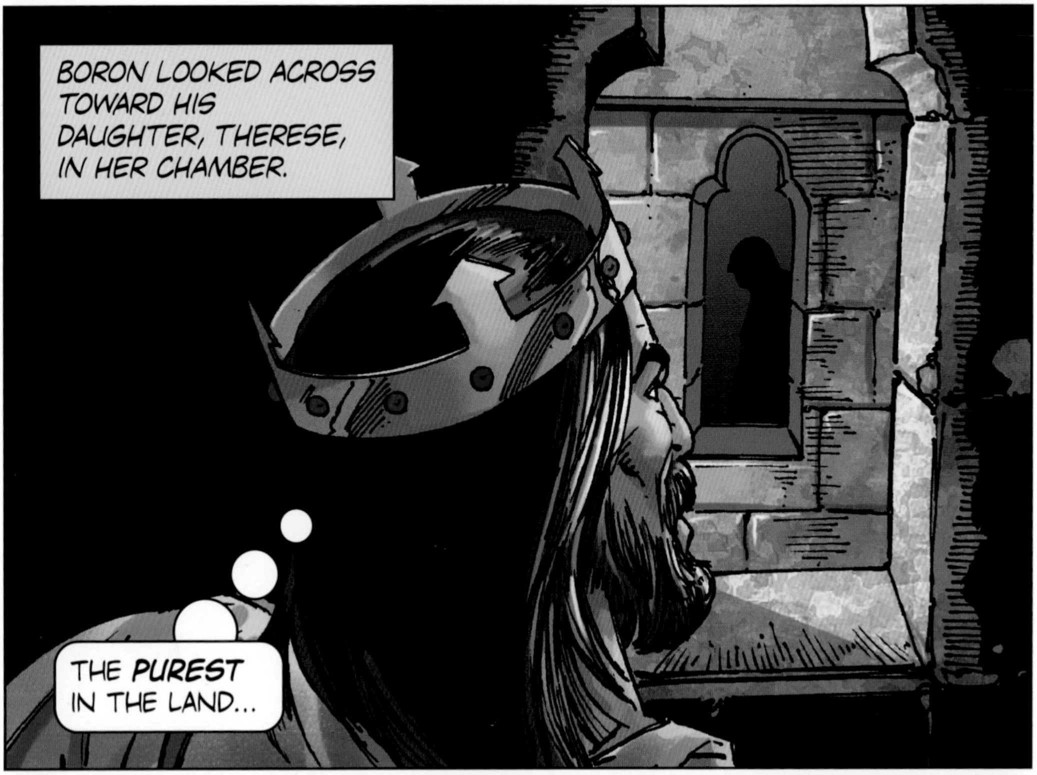
BORON LOOKED ACROSS TOWARD HIS DAUGHTER, THERESE, IN HER CHAMBER.
THE PUREST IN THE LAND...

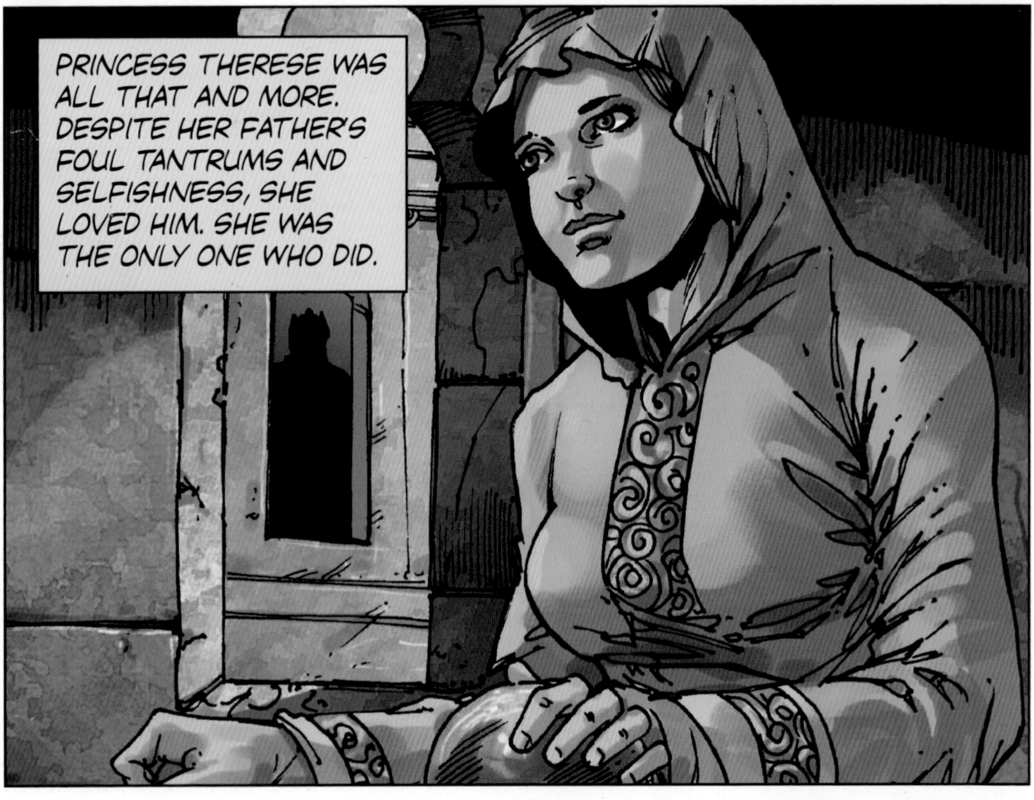
PRINCESS THERESE WAS ALL THAT AND MORE. DESPITE HER FATHER'S FOUL TANTRUMS AND SELFISHNESS, SHE LOVED HIM. SHE WAS THE ONLY ONE WHO DID.

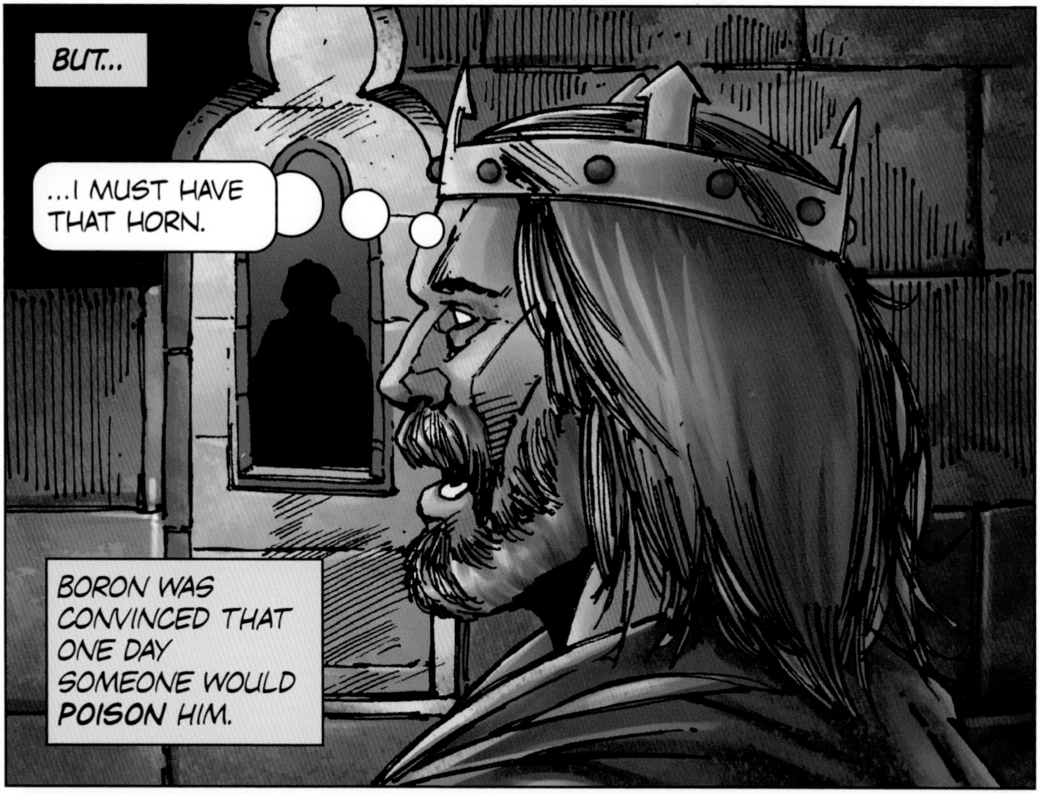
BUT...
...I MUST HAVE THAT HORN.
BORON WAS CONVINCED THAT ONE DAY SOMEONE WOULD **POISON** HIM.

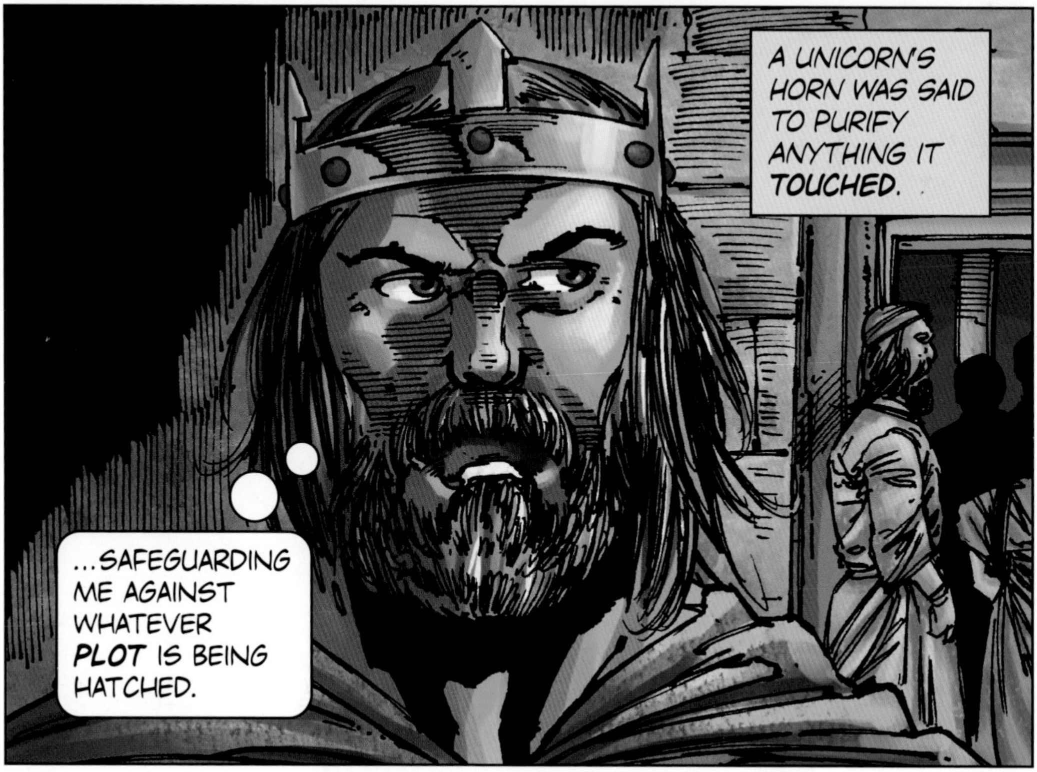
A UNICORN'S HORN WAS SAID TO PURIFY ANYTHING IT **TOUCHED**.
...SAFEGUARDING ME AGAINST WHATEVER **PLOT** IS BEING HATCHED.

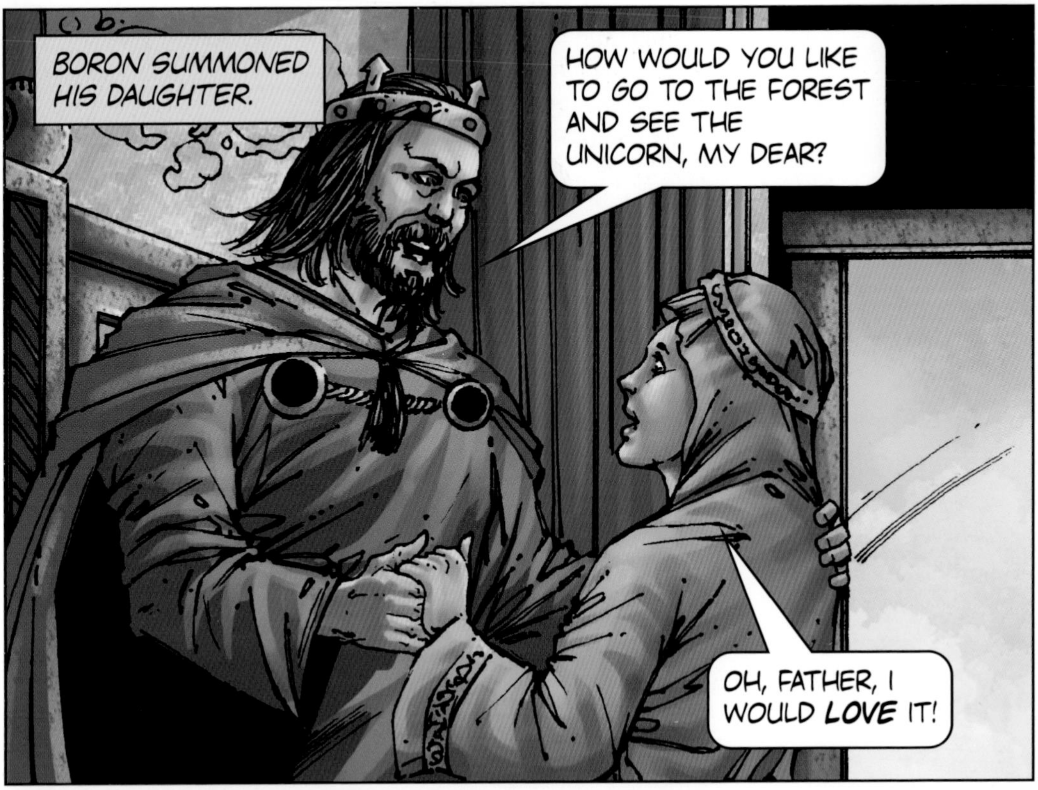
BORON SUMMONED HIS DAUGHTER.
HOW WOULD YOU LIKE TO GO TO THE FOREST AND SEE THE UNICORN, MY DEAR?
OH, FATHER, I WOULD LOVE IT!

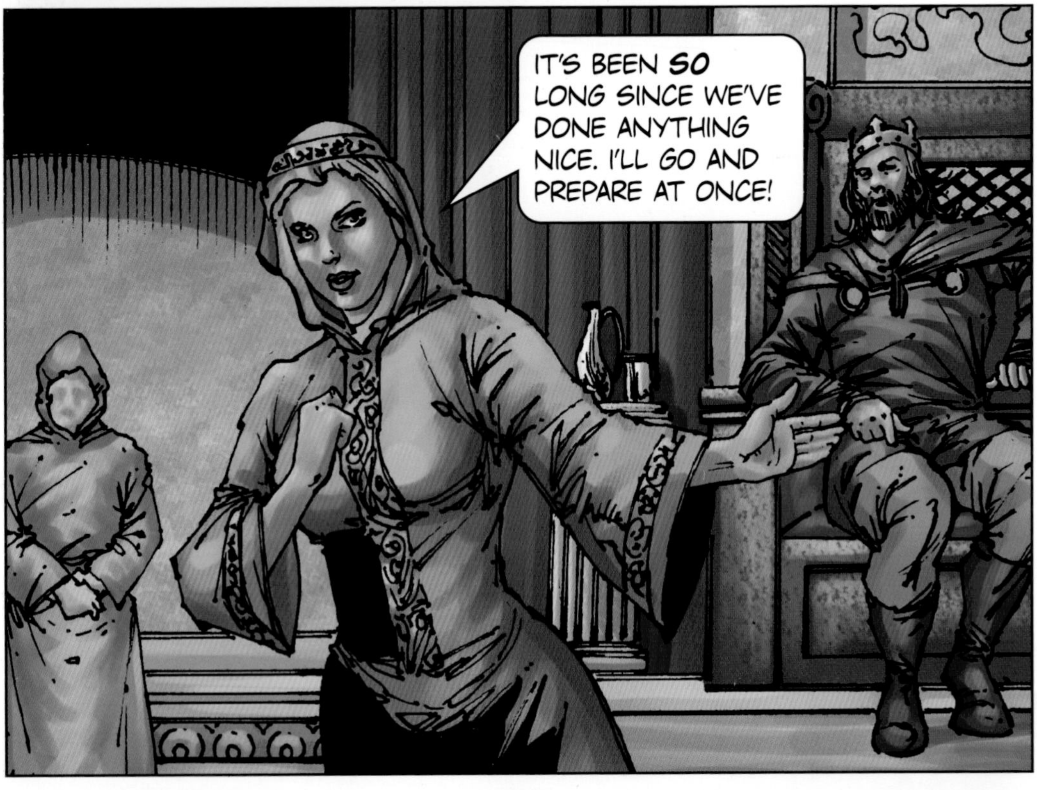
IT'S BEEN SO LONG SINCE WE'VE DONE ANYTHING NICE. I'LL GO AND PREPARE AT ONCE!

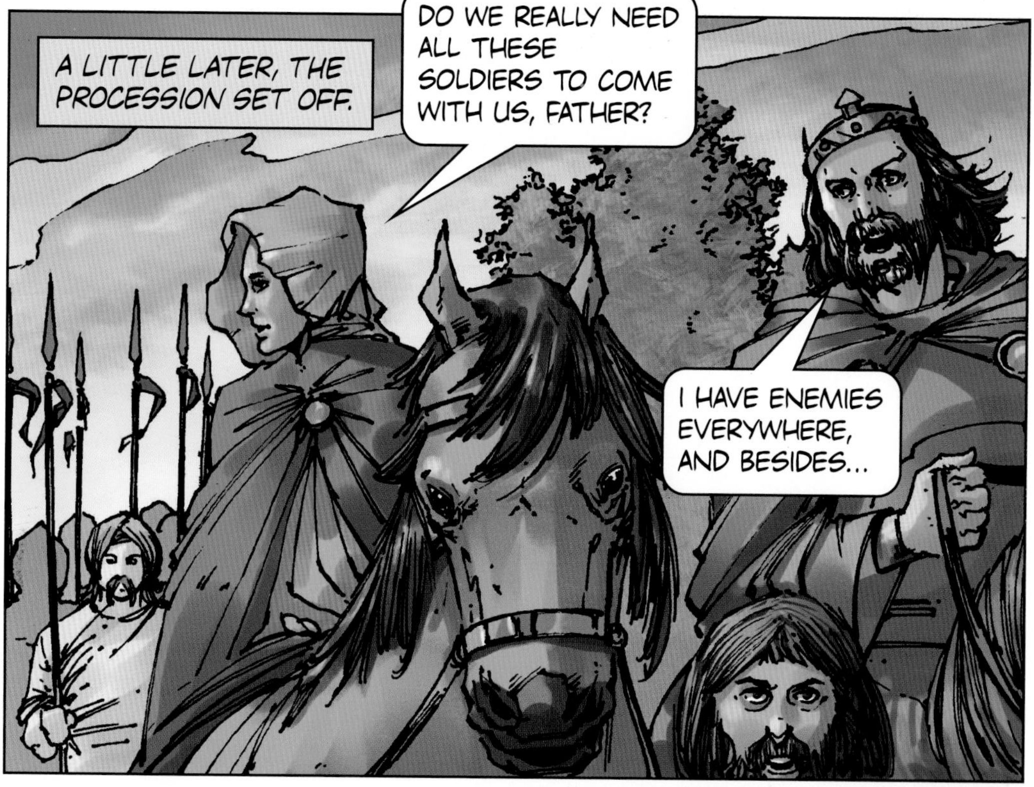
A LITTLE LATER, THE PROCESSION SET OFF.
DO WE REALLY NEED ALL THESE SOLDIERS TO COME WITH US, FATHER?
I HAVE ENEMIES EVERYWHERE, AND BESIDES...

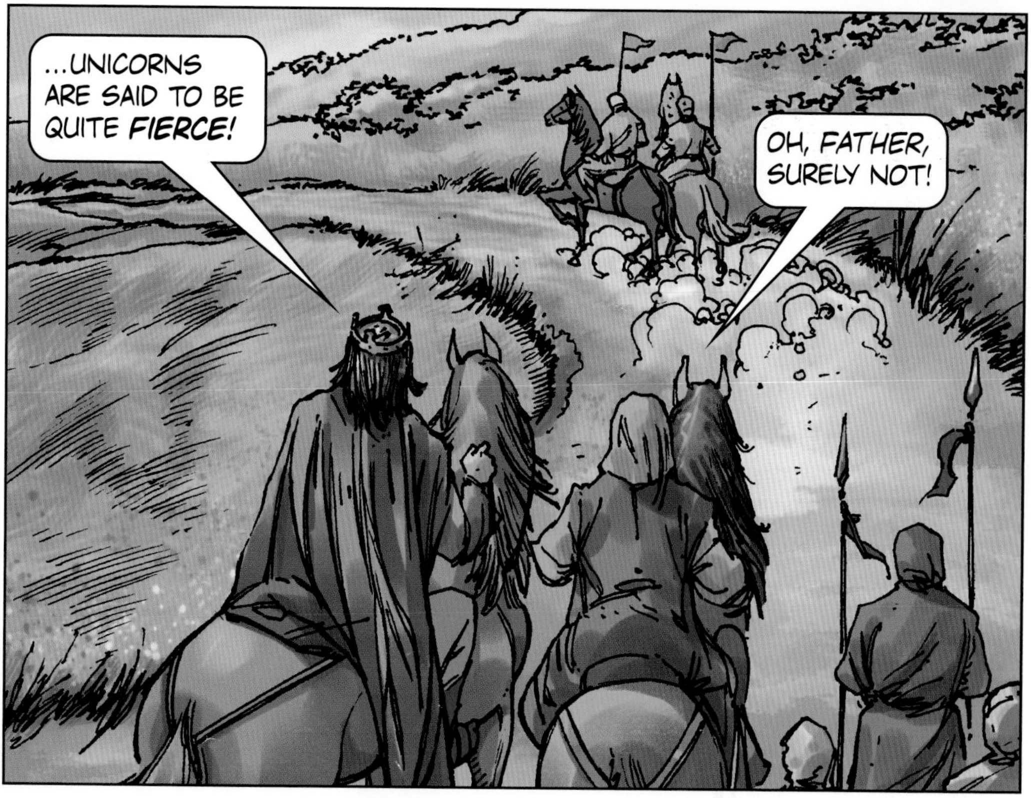
...UNICORNS ARE SAID TO BE QUITE ***FIERCE!***
OH, FATHER, SURELY NOT!

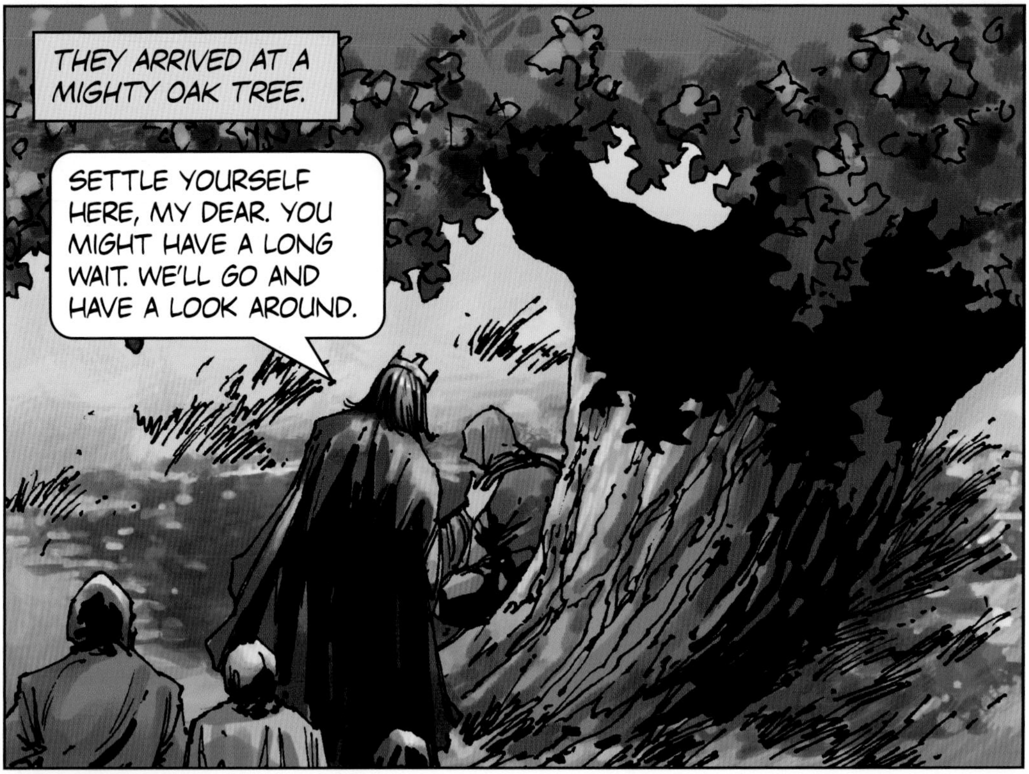
THEY ARRIVED AT A MIGHTY OAK TREE.
SETTLE YOURSELF HERE, MY DEAR. YOU MIGHT HAVE A LONG WAIT. WE'LL GO AND HAVE A LOOK AROUND.

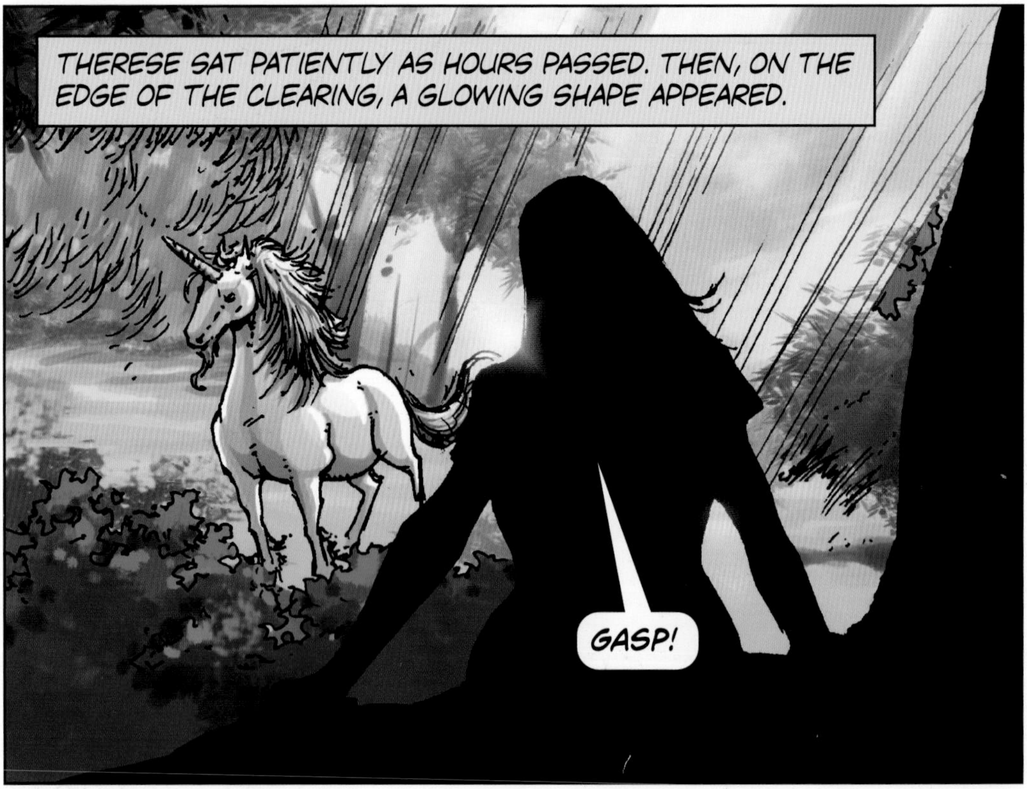
THERESE SAT PATIENTLY AS HOURS PASSED. THEN, ON THE EDGE OF THE CLEARING, A GLOWING SHAPE APPEARED.
GASP!

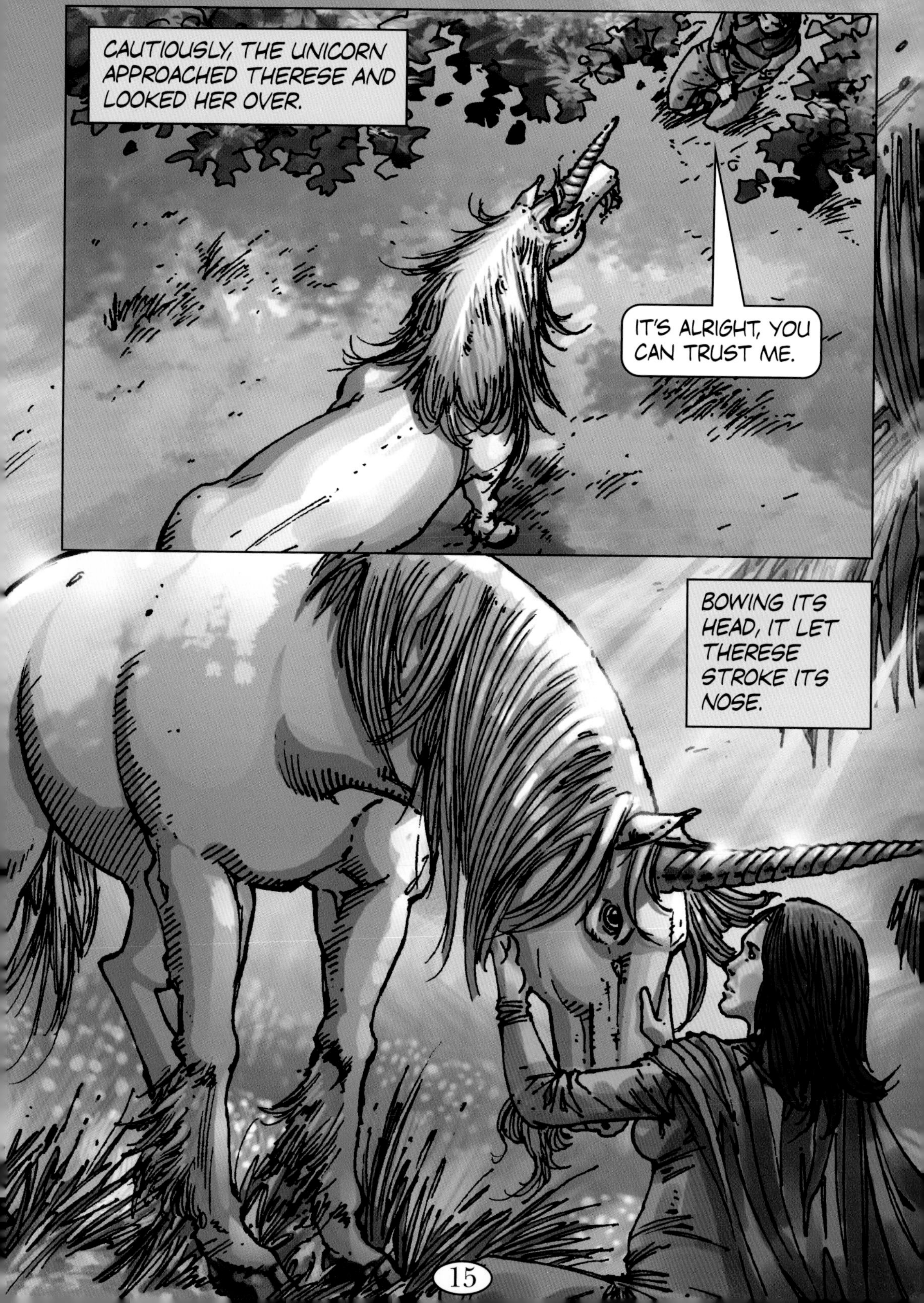
CAUTIOUSLY, THE UNICORN APPROACHED THERESE AND LOOKED HER OVER.
IT'S ALRIGHT, YOU CAN TRUST ME.
BOWING ITS HEAD, IT LET THERESE STROKE ITS NOSE.

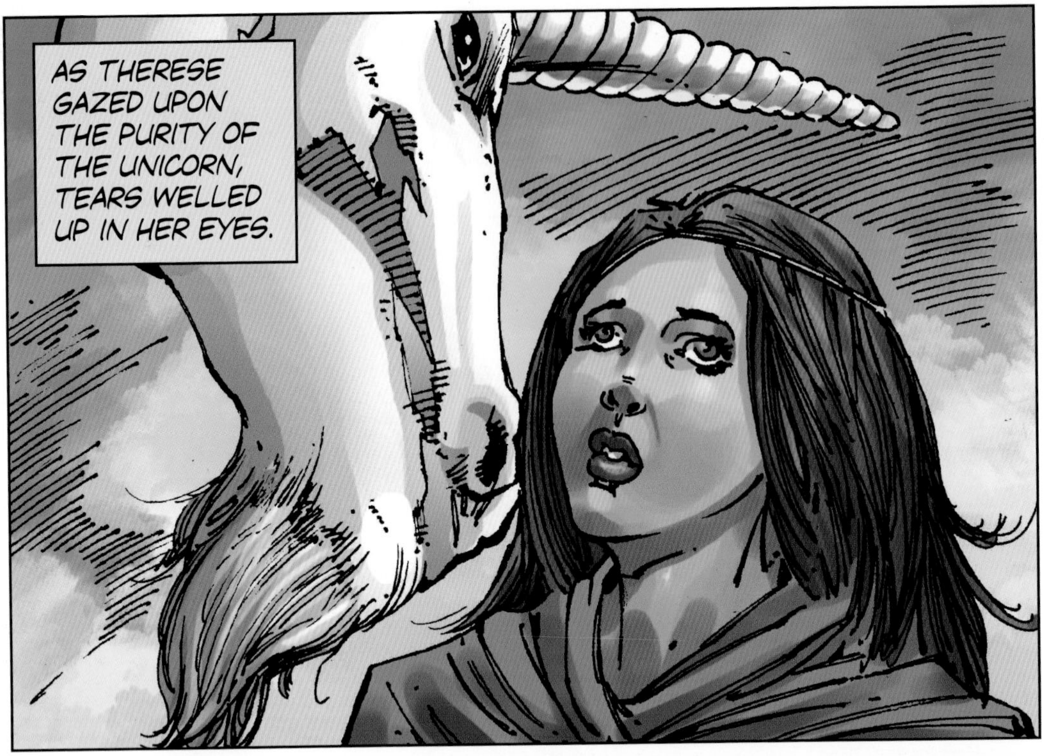
AS THERESE GAZED UPON THE PURITY OF THE UNICORN, TEARS WELLED UP IN HER EYES.

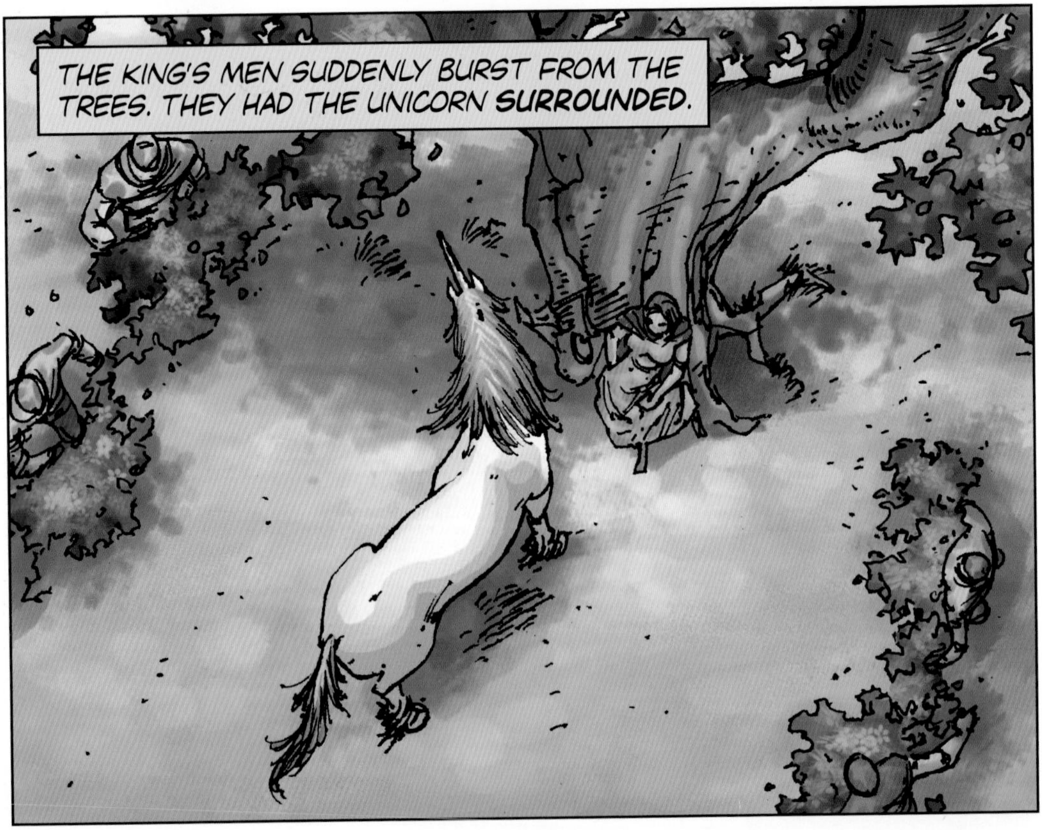
THE KING'S MEN SUDDENLY BURST FROM THE TREES. THEY HAD THE UNICORN **SURROUNDED**.

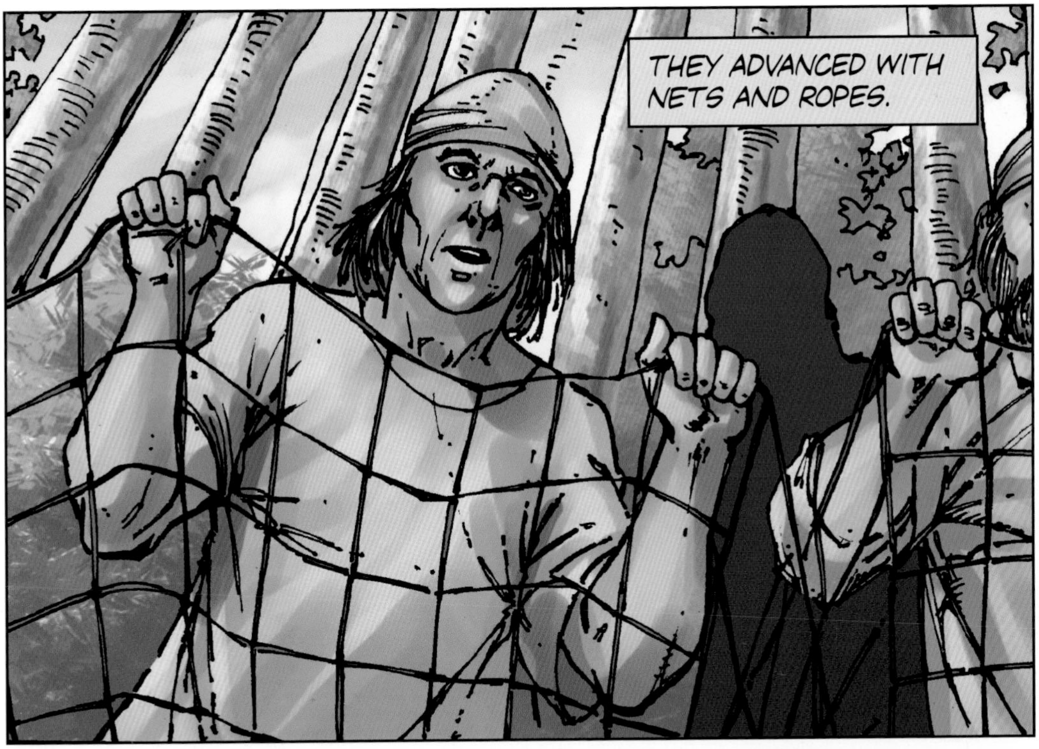
THEY ADVANCED WITH NETS AND ROPES.

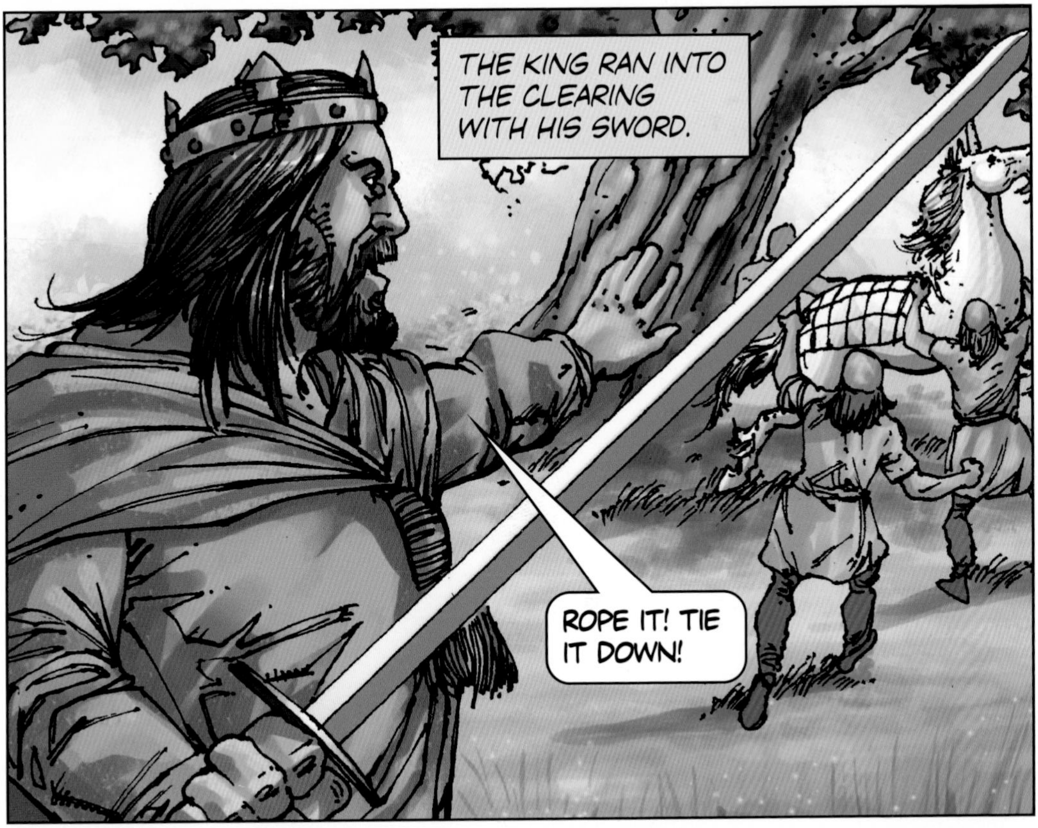
THE KING RAN INTO THE CLEARING WITH HIS SWORD.
ROPE IT! TIE IT DOWN!

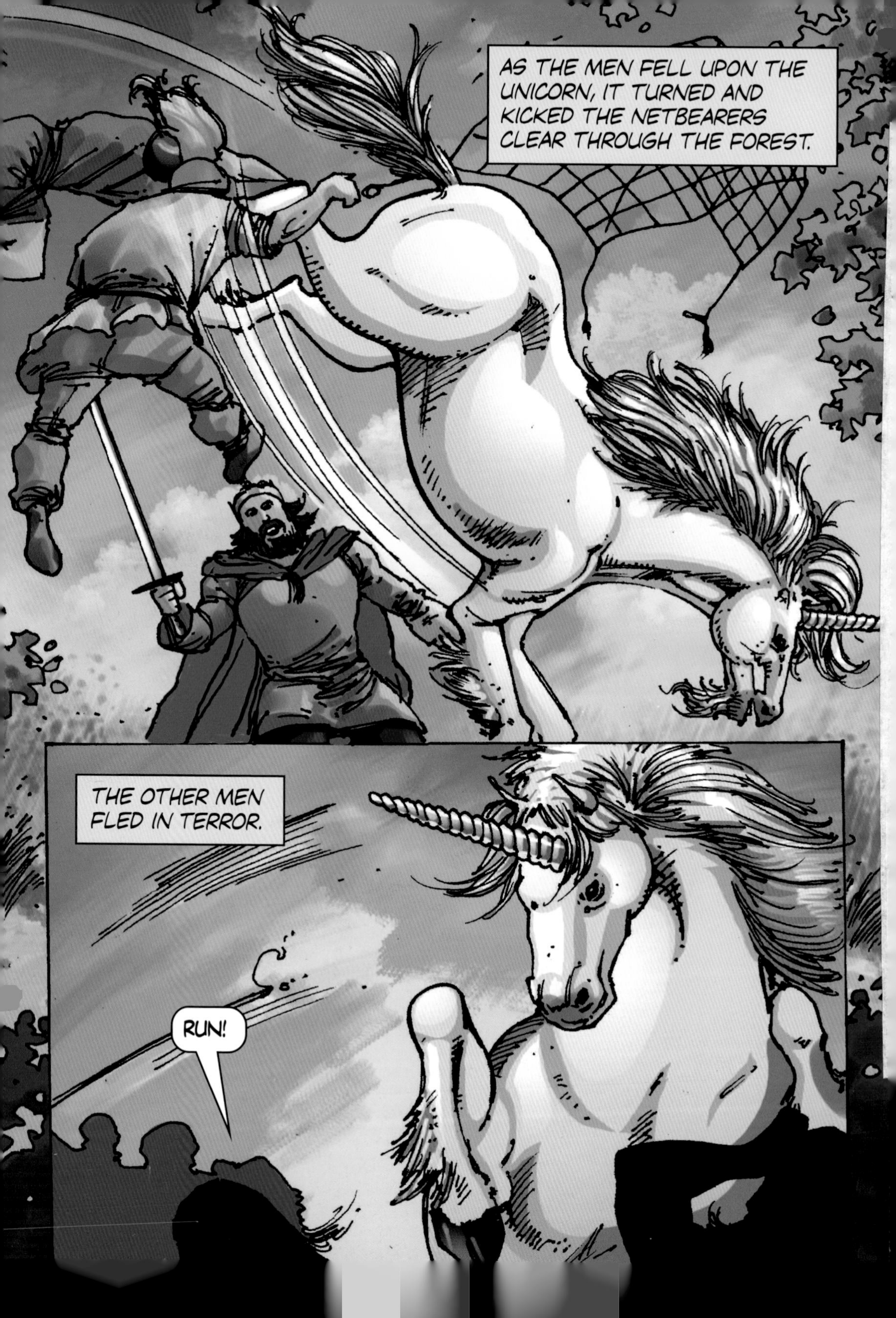
AS THE MEN FELL UPON THE UNICORN, IT TURNED AND KICKED THE NETBEARERS CLEAR THROUGH THE FOREST.
THE OTHER MEN FLED IN TERROR.
RUN!

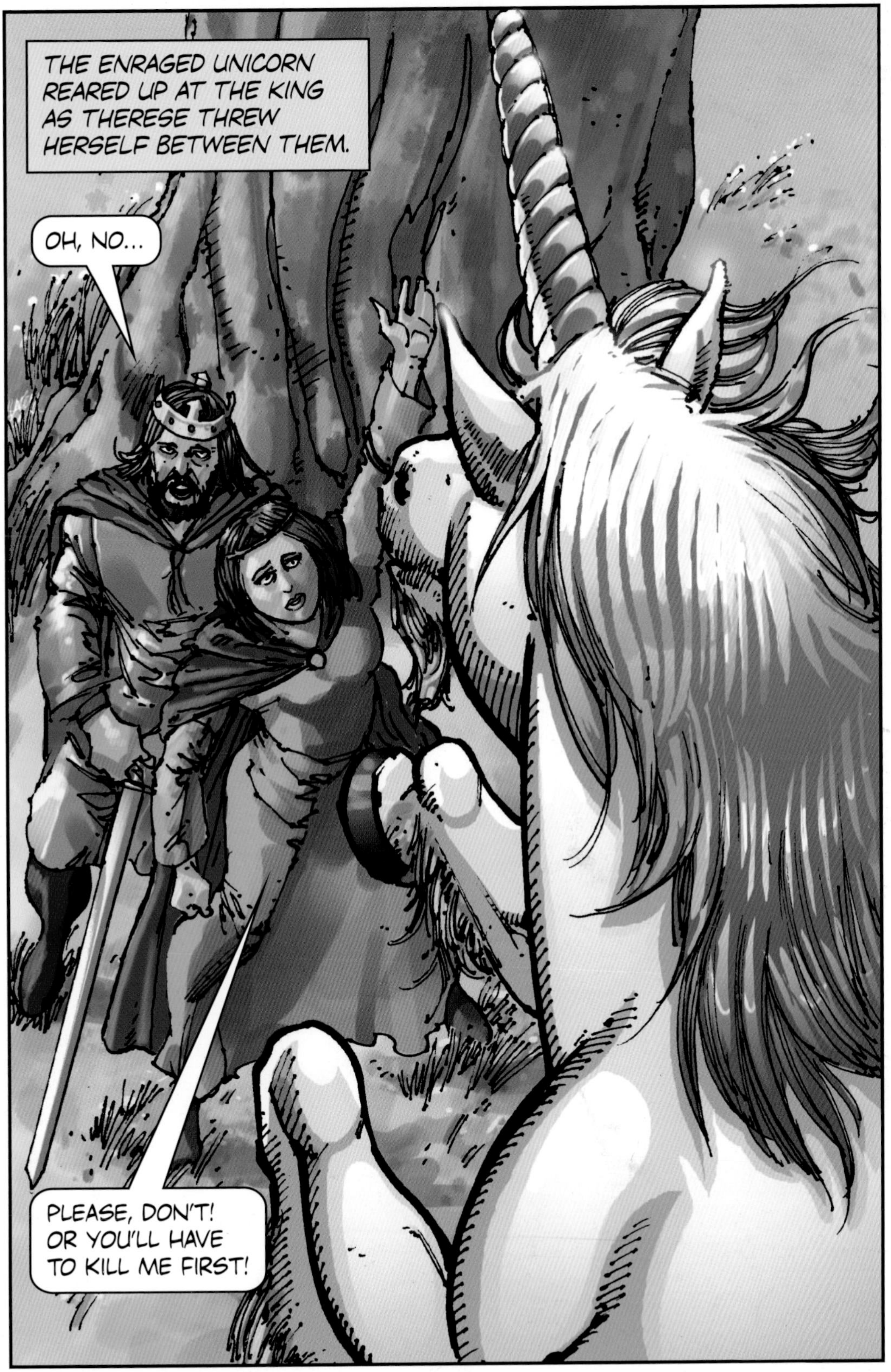
THE ENRAGED UNICORN REARED UP AT THE KING AS THERESE THREW HERSELF BETWEEN THEM.
OH, NO...
PLEASE, DON'T! OR YOU'LL HAVE TO KILL ME FIRST!

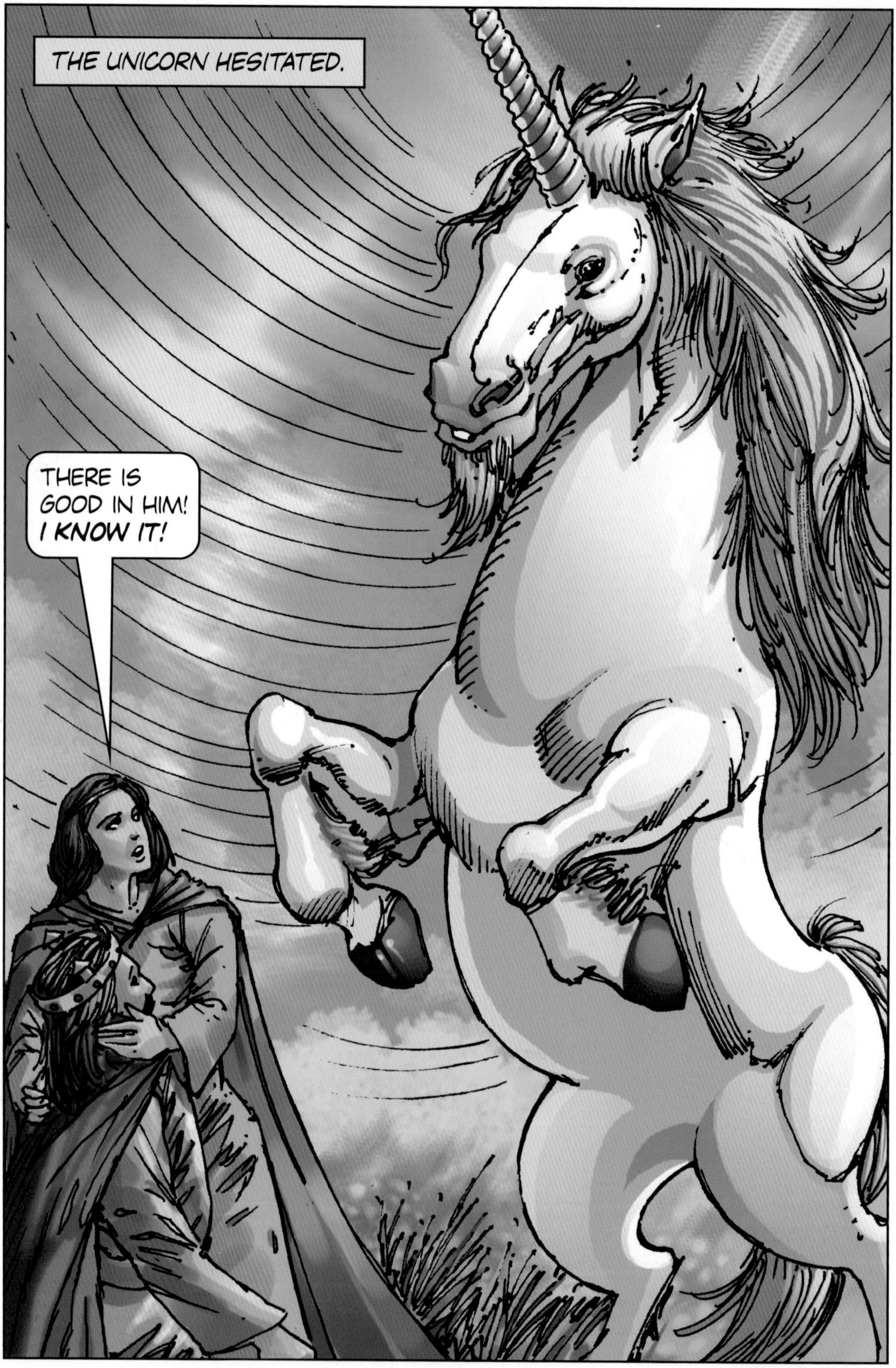
THE UNICORN HESITATED.
THERE IS GOOD IN HIM! I KNOW IT!

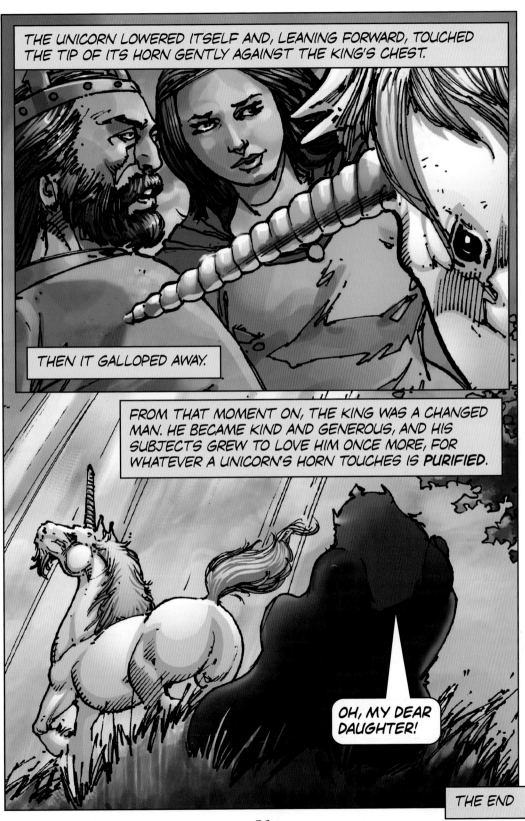

THE UNICORN LOWERED ITSELF AND, LEANING FORWARD, TOUCHED THE TIP OF ITS HORN GENTLY AGAINST THE KING'S CHEST.

THEN IT GALLOPED AWAY.

FROM THAT MOMENT ON, THE KING WAS A CHANGED MAN. HE BECAME KIND AND GENEROUS, AND HIS SUBJECTS GREW TO LOVE HIM ONCE MORE, FOR WHATEVER A UNICORN'S HORN TOUCHES IS **PURIFIED**.

OH, MY DEAR DAUGHTER!

THE END

More Unicorn Tales

Even as late as the 18th century, many in the West still believed unicorns were real, so there are far fewer legends about them compared to other mythical animals. Meanwhile, in the East, unicorn-like creatures had been haunting mythological bestiaries for centuries…

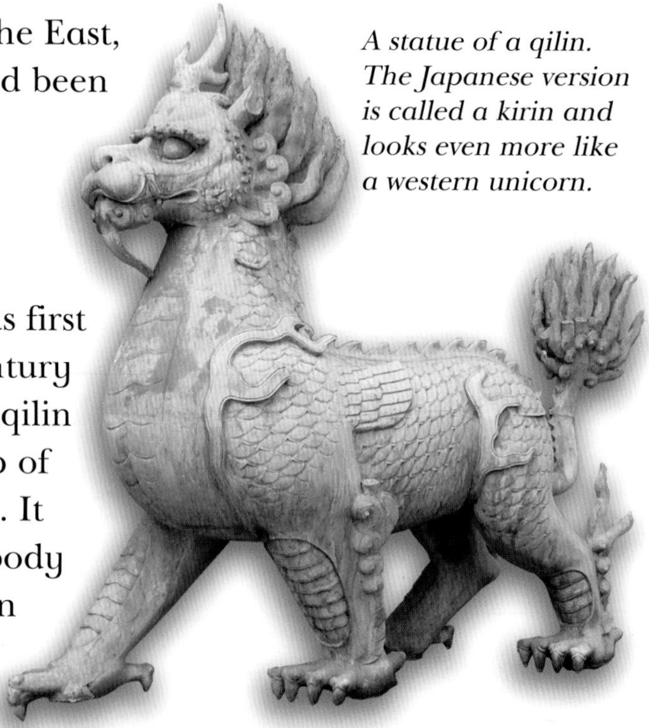

A statue of a qilin. The Japanese version is called a kirin and looks even more like a western unicorn.

The Qilin

This Chinese creature was first mentioned in the 3rd century BC. Like the unicorn, the qilin was a chimera—made up of parts from other animals. It had two horns, a deer's body with horses' hoofs, and an ox's tail. The colorful, yellow-bellied, and rainbow-backed qilin was so gentle it would even refuse to trample fresh grass. It would appear at the birth or death of a sage or king, but only if they were kind.

The Unicorns and Noah's Ark

The story tells how the proud unicorns refused to enter the ark, preferring to swim. As they swam in the great waters, birds swooped down to rest on their horns, drowning them. This is why there are no unicorns in the world today.

King Arthur and the Unicorn

Young King Arthur, stranded on a distant shore, enlists the help of a giant to free his boat. The twist is that the giant is the son of a dwarf, but was raised by a unicorn after the dwarf's wife died in childbirth. The unicorn's milk made the boy grow huge.

GLOSSARY

bestiaries Collections of fables about real and mythical animals.

chivalry The rules of knighthood, which include courtesy and generosity.

cloven Split, divided.

hesitated Paused, stopped before acting.

lore Common knowledge or wisdom on a subject.

lured Attracted or tempted by some type of reward.

narwhal A small whale with a long, spiral tusk.

neutralize To make something ineffective or not able to work.

purify To make free from dirt, evil, or guilt.

Renaissance A period of time in Europe from the 14th to 17th centuries during which art, literature, and learning underwent a great revival and marked the transition from the Middle Ages to the modern world.

uarding Protecting, defending, keeping from harm.

ned Called to appear in a particular place, such as a court.

Index